how to ruin your life

and other lessons school doesn't teach you

how to ruin your life

your life

and other lessons school doesn't teach you

Carolyn McTighe

Red Deer PRESS

Published by
Red Deer Press
A Fitzhenry & Whiteside Company
195 Allstate Parkway,
Markham, ON L3R 4T8
www.reddeerpress.com

Edited by Peter Carver
Cover design and text design by Tanya Montini
Cover image Hill Street Studios. Coffee stain image on page 6 by Tanya Montini
Printed and bound in Canada

Red Deer Press acknowledges with thanks the Canada Council for the Arts,
and the Ontario Arts Council for their support of our publishing program.
We acknowledge the financial support of the Government of Canada through the
Book Publishing Industry Development Program (BPIDP) for our publishing activities.

**Canada Council
for the Arts** **Conseil des Arts
du Canada**

**ONTARIO ARTS COUNCIL
CONSEIL DES ARTS DE L'ONTARIO**

Library and Archives Canada Cataloguing in Publication
McTighe, Carolyn
How to ruin your life / Carolyn McTighe.
ISBN 978-0-88995-401-4
I. Title.
PS8625.T55H58 2010   jC813'.6   C2010-900196-6

Publisher Cataloging-in-Publication Data (U.S)
McTighe, Carolyn.
How to ruin your life / Carolyn McTighe.
[160] p. : cm.
ISBN: 978-0-88995-401-4 (pbk.)
1. Friendships Juvenile fiction. 2. Interpersonal relations Juvenile fiction. I. Title.

[Fic] dc22 PZ7.M3854Ho 2010

Mixed Sources
Product group from well-managed
forests, controlled sources and
recycled wood or fiber
www.fsc.org Cert no. SW-COC-002358
© 1996 Forest Stewardship Council

ANCIENT FOREST ™
FRIENDLY

To my wonderful husband

and four beautiful children.

lesson ①

Hi Katie,

Here's my list. I worked on it last night after I finished my math homework. I really don't like having Ms. Watkins for a teacher this year. She's always giving us lots of homework to do. Sometimes I wish were back in Mrs. Sordie's class. It was so easy. All we ever did was paint pictures and watch those weird nature movies. I can't wait to read your list. I'm going to try to read it during morning announcements. See you at recess.

Your best friend in the whole world,
P.J.

A List of Penelope Jane Parker's Likes and Dislikes

1. I really, really like my best friend Katie. We're going to be best friends forever. Even when we're super old and our hair starts to turn gray. I think that happens when you're in your thirties or something, because my mom's always coloring her hair.

2. I don't like bananas. They are too squishy and smooshy, not to mention they get all brown and slimy when you forget to take them out of your backpack.

3. I only like pizza with pineapple and anchovies on it. Mom thinks it's gross, but I told her that she'd probably like it if she tried it. Mom said she wouldn't eat it if her life depended on it. She can be pretty dramatic sometimes.

4. I don't like turnips. Last Christmas, my mom made mashed turnip casserole, and after I ate some, I threw up all over Uncle Jim's lap. Yuck!

5. I really like the color pink. Green used to be my favorite color, until David Franco told me I looked like a giant booger last Tuesday when I wore my favorite green T-shirt to school. Boys can be such jerks!

6. I don't like my next door neighbor's dog Violet. She barks all the time, and whenever Mrs. Grimson takes her for a walk, she lets Violet poop on the sidewalk. Yesterday, on my way home from school, I stepped in Violet's poop and ruined my new runners. Mom didn't even want to wash my shoes. She said that it was disgusting and that Mrs. Grimson should be ashamed of herself. I think she threw them in the garbage. Now I have to wear my old runners.

7. I like (actually, love) pickled beet sandwiches with the crusts cut off. Dad told me that my taste in sandwiches is quite "ek-sen-trik." I'm not really sure what that means. I asked my brother and he told me that it means Mom and Dad think I'm weird. I'm pretty sure he's lying.

Hi P.J.,

Sorry about the coffee stain. I accidentally left my list on the kitchen counter last night and Mom spilled her coffee on it. We used a hairdryer to dry it off, but the stain didn't go away. I think next time we're going to have to write lists about something else, because I'm running out of things I like and don't like. Can our next list be about jobs we want to have when we're older? I already know exactly what my number one job would be. Don't let Ms. Watkins catch you reading my list this time. Remember what happened last week ... d-e-t-e-n-t-i-o-n! Meet you at the swings at recess.

Your best friend,
Katie

A List of Katie Brewer's Likes and Dislikes

1. I like my best friend, P.J. When we get older, we're going to get an apartment together and open our own veterinarian clinic.

2. I don't like gym class. Usually I don't mind gym, but right now we're doing square dancing and my partner's Jared King. Jared's hands are always sweaty! I'd tell him to dry them off but I don't want to hurt his feelings.

3. I really like my mom's homemade chocolate chip cookies. I'm actually eating one right now, so that's why I thought of it.

4. I don't like my new haircut. I know you said that it makes me look older, but I think I look dumb. My mom made the hairdresser give me bangs. I haven't had bangs since I was four years old. Mom says I look like a young Dorothy Hamill, whoever that is.

5. I like visiting my dad. This summer, Dad has promised to take me to London. He told me that he thinks I'm really going to like it there. I kind of wish we were going by ourselves, but Rachel, his new wife, will be coming too. Shoot!

6. I don't like running. This year's track meet is only a few days away, and I'm already dreading the thought of having to compete. Why can't they have contests for things I'm good at, like eating pizza or jumping rope? I wish I didn't have to enter any of the races. Then I could just focus all my energy on cheering for you.

lesson

②

*M*y name is Penelope Jane Parker and I am nine years old. My dad says I was named after my great-great grandmother because I have red hair and freckles just like she did. It's a nice story, but it doesn't change the fact that I hate my name. Dogs, pigs, and cows are named Penelope, not nine-year-old girls. When I was five, I asked my parents if I could change my name to Jane. Dad said that when I got older I'd appreciate how unique my name is, but I told him I'd appreciate it even more if I could change it to Beth, Mary, or Kelly. They said no. We decided to compromise. I couldn't change my name, but from that day forward I could go by P.J.

When I'm not at home, I'm in the fourth grade at Wellington Elementary. My teacher's name is Ms. Watkins, and I really like her because she smells nice and wears glasses just like me. The only thing I don't like about Ms. Watkins is that she's always giving us homework. She's some sort of homework fanatic. We even had homework over Christmas! My best friend Katie and I think she probably doesn't sleep much at night, because she's too busy coming up with new homework assignments.

*T*oday at school, our principal, Mr. Smilie, announced over the loudspeaker that next Tuesday was track-and-field day. I was so excited because it's my favorite day of the entire year. We don't have to do any schoolwork, and we get to eat hot dogs and chips all day long. We also get to compete in a bunch of different events, and if you're really good, you can even win a ribbon. Last year, I won two second-place ribbons and one for first place. Mom was so proud she left them hanging on the fridge for over a month. My best event is probably the hundred-meter sprint. That's the race I won my blue ribbon in last year. Actually, I've won first place in that race every year since the first grade. My dad says it's because I'm a natural athlete. I'm not sure what that is, but I plan on winning it this year, too.

When the recess bell finally rang, I ran over to Katie's locker. I couldn't wait to tell her how excited I was.

"Aren't you excited about track-and-field day?" I asked.

"Not really," Katie said, shaking her head.

"Oh, I am!" I exclaimed. "It's the greatest day ever! I think this year I'm gonna wear my lucky purple track shorts with the pink stripe down the side. They make me run faster."

"Of course *you'd* like it!" Katie said. "You've never lost a race. If I won all the time, I'd like track day, too."

I could tell from the look on Katie's face that she felt bad. Since the first grade, Katie's only ever won one ribbon. It was for long jump, and she won it because the girl she was competing against twisted her ankle.

"I'm sure you'll win something this year," I said. I was trying my best to be helpful. "You're good at lots of stuff."

Katie took a deep breath and rolled her eyes. "Like what?"

"Like ..." I thought really hard. "Like ... high jump. You're really good at high jump. In fact, I bet this year you come in first place."

"That's funny," she said. "Because last year I didn't even make it over the bar."

"Yeah, well, you've probably grown a few inches since then," I said. "All the best high jumpers are tall."

"Whatever," she shrugged.

After recess Ms. Watkins took our class down to the gym to practice for the track meet. Katie was a bit happier when she realized she wasn't going to have to promenade around the gym holding Jared King's sweaty hands. After we did a few stretches and twisty things that made me feel dizzy, the boys were put into one group and the girls were put into another.

"I would like the boys to line up behind the high jump," Ms. Watkins said. "Girls, I would like you to get into groups of four. Each group will run one lap around the track. The winners in each race will then compete against each other."

Ms. Watkins looked over her shoulder to where the boys were trying to line up. Benjamin Peterson was hanging off one of the ropes, pretending to be a monkey.

"I'll be back to start the race as soon as I get the boys started on the high jump," Ms. Watkins explained. She pushed her sliding glasses back up onto the bridge of her nose.

Once she left, I raced over to Katie and grabbed her by the arm.

"We'll be in a group together!" I whispered.

Katie didn't answer. I could tell she was still upset, so I decided I wouldn't try that hard at practice and would let her win. After all, it was just practice, and maybe beating me would give her more confidence. Jennifer Andrews and Heather Fisher joined our group. I wasn't too worried about them beating Katie, because they seemed more interested in what the boys were doing than winning any sort of race.

"Okay, girls," Ms. Watkins called, after returning from looking after the boys. "I want you all to line up in your groups behind P.J."

*M*y group was going to run first and I could hardly keep still. Even though I planned to let Katie win, I decided that I would run as fast as I could for the first bit and then slow down near the finish line, so Katie could catch up and then pass me. After all, I couldn't just lose right off the bat; Katie would know something was up.

"On your mark. Get set … go!" Ms. Watkins shouted.

We were off. Just as I had suspected, Jennifer and Heather were no challenge whatever. They practically walked around the gym and didn't once take their eyes off the boys.

"Heather and Jennifer!" Ms. Watkins hollered. "I want to see you two put some effort into this race!"

As I made my way around the first bend, I looked back to see where Katie was.

I was surprised to see her only a few feet behind me, totally keeping up. For a second, I thought maybe my feet had decided to slow down before my brain gave them permission to. I turned and tried to run faster, but the harder I tried the more I realized my legs couldn't move any quicker. I was running as fast as I could, and Katie was still gaining on me.

"Way to go, Katie!" Ms. Watkins yelled. "Keep it up! You're almost there!"

Suddenly, Katie was right beside me. When I looked over

at her, she shrugged her shoulders and smiled her biggest smile. I think she was just as surprised as I was.

"Isn't this great?" she said. "I don't know what happened."

"Yeah," I said. I was completely out of breath. "You're … (puff) … doing great! Have … (puff) … you been … (puff) … practicing or … (puff) … something?"

"No!" she answered. "I had a bowl of oatmeal for breakfast this morning, but that's about it."

"It … (puff) … must be … (puff) … the oatmeal," I said. "Dad … (puff) … says it's … (puff) … really good … (puff) … for you and … (puff) … everything."

"I guess so," she said. And with that, she was gone.

For the next few moments, I watched Katie make her way around the last bend of the track toward the finish line. Ms. Watkins was clapping her hands really hard. I could tell she was happy for Katie, because Katie doesn't usually do that well in gym. Last month, during floor hockey, Katie scored six times on her own goal. And the month before that, she accidentally gave Hugh Maxwell a bloody nose when she hit him in the face with a basketball … and he was sitting in the bleachers.

When Katie finally crossed the finish line, Ms. Watkins and a few of the girls ran over to her and began patting her on the back. I wanted to run over, too, but I still had a long way to go before I crossed the finish line. I was so proud of Katie. She had finally found something in gym class that she was good at! And that's when it hit me. If Katie could beat me in a practice race, then she could probably beat me at the real thing, too. And if she could beat me at the real thing, then I wouldn't be the fastest girl in the fourth grade anymore. And if I weren't the fastest girl in the fourth grade anymore, then I wouldn't win the first-place ribbon at the track meet next Tuesday. And if I didn't win the first-place ribbon at the track meet next Tuesday, then Mom wouldn't have anything to hang on the fridge. And if Mom didn't have anything to hang on the fridge, then she wouldn't have any reason to be proud of me.

As I crossed the finish line, Katie walked up to me and grabbed me by the arm. She was still grinning from ear to ear about her big win.

"P.J.," she said. "Can you believe it? I actually beat you in a race!"

"I know," I said. "You don't have to rub it in."

"I'm not," Katie answered. "I'm just so excited! Ms. Watkins even said that she couldn't believe I ran as fast as I did. I told her it was probably the oatmeal, like you said. She laughed when I told her that."

"That's great!" I said. I only half meant it.

"Now I know why you like running so much," she said. "It feels great when you win."

"Well, I don't like it anymore," I grunted. "In fact, I hate it."

Katie looked surprised. I think she knew I was lying, because my eyes started to get all watery. And the more I thought of the track meet the harder it got to hold back my tears.

"You don't have to cry about it," Katie said.

"I'm not! I just have an eyelash in my eye."

I didn't want to be mad at Katie, but I couldn't help it. How could she take away the only thing I was good at? I wasn't walking around beating her at the things she did well, like roller-skating and fractions. No matter how hard I tried, I couldn't help feeling bad. It was, officially, the worst day of my life.

lesson 3

When the bell finally rang at the end of the day, I rushed out of the classroom and headed straight for my locker. I had decided after gym class that Katie and I just couldn't be friends anymore. There isn't enough room in our relationship for two athletes. Not to mention the fact that ever since she beat me during practice, she's been impossible to be around.

"Hey, wait up!" Katie hollered, running over to my locker.

I pretended like I didn't hear her. I figured the silent treatment would make it clear that we were no longer friends. I shut my locker door really loud, like people do in the movies when they're mad at each other, except I haven't ever seen a movie where someone slams a locker door, so I think I may be the first person to do that!

"Are you mad at me or something?" Katie asked. "You've been acting kinda weird since lunch. Is everything okay?"

"I'm fine," I said. "You're the one who's acting weird."

"No, I'm not!" Katie frowned. "I happen to know that you told everyone in the class that I farted during lunch, even though it was your smelly egg salad sandwich. I could have gotten mad, but I figured you were still pretty upset about gym class."

"Why would I be mad about gym class?" I yelled. "And just for your information, I didn't tell anyone that you farted … everyone just assumed it was you."

"You're mad because I beat you, and you can't stand the fact that I ran faster than you," Katie said.

"You actually think that you beat me?" I laughed. "You didn't beat me, I let you win!"

"Whatever!" Katie said. "I could tell you were running as fast as you could, because you could hardly talk during the race."

"Haven't you ever heard of acting?" I sputtered. "I *was* the winner of the Wellington Elementary Acting Award, after all."

"You got that stupid award when we were in Kindergarten," Katie said. "And the only reason you got it was because you peed your pants during rehearsal, and Mrs. Mercer said she'd give it to you if you promised not to do it during the show!"

"Katie Brewer!" I shouted. "I don't want to be friends with you anymore!"

"That's fine with me," Katie hollered back. "I don't want to be friends with you, either! Miss Crybaby!"

"Oh, yeah," I shouted. "Well … well … I'm gonna beat the pants off you at the track meet, and then we'll see who the crybaby is!"

"Well, you're going to need more than your lucky purple shorts to beat me, Penelope Jane Parker!" Katie said, and she slammed her locker door.

"Oh, that's original!" I mocked. "I totally invented the locker slamming thing. You're such a copycat, Katie!"

Katie stuck out her tongue. I knew she was really mad, because the only other time I've seen her do that was in the third grade when Jerald Jackson hit her in the head with a dodge ball. I rolled my eyes (Mom says I'm an expert at it) and then headed for the door.

On the way home, I started to get a strange feeling in my stomach. It wasn't a pain or the butterfly feeling you get when you're nervous, but more like a sad ache. It sort of felt like the time my mom accidentally vacuumed up my pet hamster, Gerald. Except I wasn't sad about Katie, I was mad, or at least I thought I was. Katie wasn't cute and fuzzy like Gerald, and she certainly didn't make the mistake of hiding under my bed on cleaning day. She had beaten me at the one thing I was good at. And she didn't even feel bad about it! Right then I decided, no matter what, I was going to have to win that race on Tuesday. All I had to do was figure out how, because my whole life in the fourth grade depended on it!

lesson

4

I didn't say much during dinner. This might have made Mom and Dad kind of nervous, because the last time I didn't say much at dinner was when I flushed an orange down the toilet. My stupid brother told me that if you flushed an orange down the toilet, a tree would grow underground and the branches would come out through the manhole covers. I actually believed him, until I did it and the orange got stuck. The toilet overflowed and it took a plumber three hours to finally get it out. I ended up getting grounded for a whole month, and Chris only got grounded for a week. He never gets in trouble for anything!

Mom put down her fork and got a serious look on her face. "Have you done something we should know about, P.J.? You've been awfully quiet tonight."

"I haven't done anything," I told her. "I just had a bad day at school, that's all."

"Did you get in trouble at school?" Dad asked.

I shook my head. "No," I said. "Me and Katie just got in a fight."

"Did you knock her lights out?" Chris said, punching the air with his fists.

"Christopher Parker!" Mom snapped. She gave him the look she gives us when we're at the grocery store and we're fighting, and she doesn't want to yell at us because all the other parents will think she's a terrible mother.

"What was the fight about?" Dad asked.

"Ms. Watkins had us run a practice race for next Tuesday's track meet," I explained. "I felt really bad for Katie because she isn't a good runner like me, so I decided to lose the race."

Mom looked confused. "So you two got in a fight because Katie found out you lost the race on purpose?"

"Not exactly," I said. "Katie actually won the race, but it was just a fluke. She had oatmeal for breakfast and I think it helped her run faster!"

Chris laughed so hard a few peas came out of his mouth and rolled across the table.

"It shouldn't matter how she won," Mom said. "It's just a race."

"It's not just a race," I told her. "It's the only thing I'm good at. If she beats me on Tuesday, you won't have any ribbons to hang on the fridge."

"We don't need ribbons to hang on the fridge," Dad said. "We're not proud of the ribbons you win, P.J. We're proud of your effort."

"And there are lots of things you're good at," Mom added.

"Yeah, like picking your nose," Chris snorted, through a mouthful of mashed potatoes.

"Chris!" Mom yelled.

I wanted to believe them, but I figured they were just telling me I was good at stuff the same way I told Katie she was. I actually think it's against the law for parents to say anything but good stuff about their kids.

"I must say," Dad interrupted, "I'm a little surprised to hear that you would let something as silly as a race get in the way of your friendship with Katie."

"Ex-friendship!" I corrected.

"Don't you think you're overreacting just a little?" Dad asked.

"Absolutely not!" I said. I just knew he'd take *her* side! He'd probably adopt her if he could.

"I think maybe you've let your pride get in the way of your better judgment," Mom added. "You didn't let things get too out of hand, did you?"

"No," I said. "I just told her I didn't want to be friends with her anymore. It's no big deal."

Mom and Dad stopped eating and looked at each other with stunned looks on their faces, sort of like the time Grandma Mary announced at her eighty-third birthday that she was going to take up waterskiing.

"I think you've made a big mistake," Dad said.

"You girls are such good friends," Mom added. "I'd hate to see you ruin that over something so minor."

"It's okay," I reassured them. "There are lots of girls I can be best friends with. Katie's not the only lobster in the tank."

"It's fish in the sea, dimwit," Chris said.

"That's enough," Dad said, giving Chris his "knock it off" glare. "Letting this go on for more than a day is far too long. First thing tomorrow morning, I want you to find Katie and I want you to tell her that you're sorry."

There was a long pause. I looked up and realized Dad was staring at me, waiting for me to answer him. I nodded my head. Dad smiled and got up from the table. Mom followed him into the kitchen, patting me gently on the head as she passed by.

"I know you'll do the right thing," she whispered.

*L*ater that night, as I sat at my desk doing my math homework, I started to think about everything Mom and Dad had said. I knew deep down that I was blowing things out of proportion. I also knew that Katie's friendship was more important to me than some stupid race. Despite all of this, I still felt angry. I was angry with Katie for winning, and I was angry that she was going to win first place at Tuesday's track meet. And even more than that, I was angry that she couldn't see how important the race was to me. I opened my desk drawer and took out a scrap piece of paper. I decided to try to come up with reasons to still be friends with Katie. If I could come up with enough, then maybe apologizing the next morning wouldn't be so bad.

Four Reasons Why I *Should* Be Katie Brewer's Friend

1. Katie's mom is a really good baker. Whenever I go over to her house, her Mom always has cookies and cupcakes for us to eat. My mom never makes things like that. She's into low-fat stuff and makes things like tofu brownies and soy cheesecake. Yuck!!!

2. Katie always sticks up for me. Once when I was in the second grade, Fiona Edwards told Mrs. Valentanuzzi that I pushed her off the monkey bars at recess, even though I didn't. Mrs. Valentanuzzi was just about to send me to the principal's office, when Katie told her what really happened. Mrs. Valentanuzzi ended up apologizing for not believing me, and Fiona got in trouble for lying.

3. Katie has a swimming pool. My parents won't buy a swimming pool. Mom says they're too much work and she doesn't need anything else to take care of.

4. Katie's way smarter than me and always helps me with my homework. She's prettier, too, and has nicer clothes. Her desk is always tidy and her hair never looks messy like mine. She has a dog named Buster, who sleeps on her bed every night, and she can spit farther than my brother Chris! Katie can whistle, play the piano, and juggle. Her teeth are straight and she has pierced ears. The only thing she couldn't do was run ... and now she can do that better than me, too!! I HATE KATIE BREWER!

That settled it. I didn't care what Mom or Dad said. I was never going to apologize to Katie.

lesson

⑤

A List of Katie Replacements

1. Claire Kippen is my first pick as my new best friend. She's really smart and always has cookies in her lunch, which must mean her mom's a good baker. She has a pet dog named Coco, and she knows how to ride her bike without using her hands. She can speak French and is really good at drawing horses. But best of all, Claire isn't a fast runner.

2. Macy Daniels is second on my list. She's really shy and doesn't talk too much, which is perfectly okay with me because I like to talk and do it almost all the time! I'm not sure if she's smart like Katie, because she never answers questions in class, and she usually works by herself when we have projects to do.

    The only problem with Macy is that she's a pretty good runner. That could be a problem!

3. Belinda Jones is my third choice. She's funny, smart, and

really bad at running. The only problem is that she's also really mean. When I was in the second grade, my mom bought me some pants that had pink hearts on the knees and red and purple stripes around the waist. I wore them to school one day and accidentally put them on backwards after gym class. Belinda told the whole class that my pants were on backwards, and everyone laughed at me. I told everyone that they were supposed to be worn like that because they came from Australia and everything there is backwards ... even the toilets!!! No one believed me, and for the rest of the day they called me "Backward P.J." On second thought, I think I'll just stick with Macy and Claire.

When school started Friday morning, I was determined to find a new best friend. I looked over my list of Katie replacements and decided to start with Claire, because she sits in front of me and I can pass her notes without Ms. Watkins noticing. We usually begin each morning with silent reading, so I knew Ms. Watkins would be busy at her desk with teacher stuff and probably wouldn't notice me passing notes to Claire. I quietly pulled a pen and piece of paper from my desk. I thought for a minute about what I would say and then began writing:

Claire,

Katie and I aren't best friends anymore, so I was wondering if you would like to be my new best friend. I'm a great best friend! I can keep secrets and I always keep my promises. On weekends, my mom sometimes lets me have sleepovers and we usually get to watch movies and eat pizza in the living room! I have a pretty big collection of stuffed animals and you can even borrow some if you want to. So if you want to be my best friend, please mark the "yes" box. Thanks.

○ Yes   ○ No

P.J. Parker

I carefully folded the paper in half and then leaned forward and tapped Claire on the back. When she turned around, she gave me a really grouchy face because I was interrupting her silent reading time. She grabbed the note from my hand and then turned around really fast so Ms. Watkins wouldn't see. When she finally handed the note back, I opened it quickly and looked at the two boxes at the bottom of the page. It read:

O *Yes*   ⊗ *No*

Dear P.J.,
Katie already asked me to be her new best friend and I said "yes." Sorry.

Claire

Katie Brewer is such a traitor!!!! I felt my face get all hot and prickly, like it does when my mom tries to be cool around my friends and says things like "totally rad" and "gag me with a spoon." She says that's how she and her friends talked when they were young. I think that was in the olden days when they didn't have things like television or electricity. I glanced over my shoulder at Katie because I was super mad and I was going to give her my mad face—when I noticed she was whispering something to Belinda Jones. They started to giggle and then looked over at me. Katie was turning the whole entire class against me! I had to find a new best friend and I had to do it fast!

With Claire and Belinda out of the picture, I had no other choice but to ask Macy Daniels. I took the note and carefully scratched off Claire's name and then wrote "Macy" over it real dark with my pencil. Then I erased what Claire had written and the "X" she had made in the "No" box and then folded the note back up. Macy sits right next to me so it was super easy giving her the note. I watched her read the note and then write something on it with her pink, fuzzy pencil. When she was done, she handed me back the note and I opened it super fast so I could read what it said. Neither of the two boxes had an "X" in them. I looked at the bottom of the note and began to read what Macy had written:

Dear P.J.,

Katie already told me about your fight and everyone thinks you're being silly!

Katie says you're just jealous because she beat you in gym class. She also told me that she'd still consider being your best friend if you said you were sorry. I still like you, but I can't be your best friend because Katie said so. Sorry.

Macy

I was so mad I wanted to scream, but instead I turned around and stuck my tongue out at Katie. She didn't see me because she was reading her book, but it made me feel good anyway. I crumpled up the note and put it in my desk. I guess I was kind of noisy, because Ms. Watkins stood up and looked right at me!

"P.J., I'd like to speak with you in the hallway," she said.

I was in big trouble, because Mrs. Watkins had the same look on her face as she did when she caught Ryan Phillips shooting spitballs at the chalkboard. I got up from my desk and followed her out into the hallway. Ms. Watkins shut the classroom door behind us, so no one could hear what she was going to say.

"Why do you think we have silent reading, P.J.?" she asked.

"So you have time to come up with more homework for us to do," I answered.

"No," she said frowning. "I give you silent reading in the morning so you can learn to work quietly and settle down before we start our school work."

"Oh," I said. I knew I'd get the answer wrong. I'm not good with pop quizzes.

"I was watching you during silent reading and noticed that instead of reading your book, you were busy passing notes," Ms. Watkins continued. "Not only were you not on task, but you also stopped Macy and Claire from being on task as well. Do you think that was fair?"

I shook my head. I knew the answer to that one!

"Do you want another detention?"

I shook my head again.

"Now, I understand that something is going on between you and Katie, but you need to take care of that during recess, lunch, or after school … not during class time! Do you understand?" Ms. Watkins asked.

"Yes," I said.

"You can go back to class now," Ms. Watkins ordered.

When I opened the door to the classroom, everyone turned around and looked at me. Jeremy Jacobs and Ryan Phillips both laughed when I walked past their desks.

"P.J. got in trouble! P.J. got in trouble!" they both whispered.

I sat down at my desk and bit the inside of my cheek really hard so I wouldn't cry.

"Are you gonna cry, P.J.?" Jeremy asked.

"P.J. Parker's a crybaby! P.J. Parker's a crybaby!" Ryan sang.

"Why don't you just leave her alone?" Katie shouted from behind me.

I turned my head around really fast, because I couldn't believe Katie was sticking up for me. It was like old times. She had finally come to her senses! I looked at her and smiled, but she didn't smile back. Instead, she stuck her nose in the air, turned her head, and started talking to Belinda Jones. I turned back around in my seat and stared at the chalkboard. It wasn't even lunchtime and I had already lost *all* my friends, gotten in trouble with Ms. Watkins, and been made fun of by the meanest boys in the fourth grade. I figured my day couldn't get any worse, except for one thing … I was totally wrong!

lesson 7

*L*unch without friends is rotten! I didn't feel like eating, even though it was my favorite: a pickled beet sandwich with the crusts cut off, a butterscotch pudding, and four dill pickles sliced down the middle. I used to eat my lunch with Katie, but since we weren't friends anymore and since she turned the whole school against me, I decided to eat alone. Katie ate her lunch with Macy, Claire, and Belinda.

Since it was Friday and we didn't have gym class, I had to figure out a way to race Katie. I decided that the only way I could do it was to follow her during lunch and race her back to the classroom when the bell rang. That way, I could prove I was still the fastest runner, and the whole school could see me beat her. So, for the whole lunch hour, I followed Katie wherever she went.

12:15 PM Followed Katie to the swings. Hid behind a tall pine tree so she wouldn't see me, and ended up getting sticky pine stuff all over my jacket. Gross!

12:20 PM Followed Katie over to the monkey bars. She swung upside down for a little while and then got down to talk to Claire and Macy. I hid behind a large blue garbage can. It was real smelly, and someone hit me in the head with a half-eaten bologna sandwich.

12:30 PM Followed Katie to her locker. She grabbed her sweater and then went back outside. I hid behind the school janitor, Mr. Kirby, while he swept the hallway. I think he thinks I'm weird!

12:40 PM Followed Katie back to the swings. Decided not to hide behind the sticky pine tree again, so instead, hid behind our lunch monitor, Mrs. Porter.

12:50 PM The school bell rang. I was still behind Mrs. Porter, so I waited until Katie was right beside me when I jumped out and started to run. I ran as fast as I could. Katie was running, too, except she kept getting farther and farther ahead of me. I ran even harder, but she was still winning! I ran so hard that I had to close my eyes to concentrate, and that's when it happened!

12:53 PM I ran straight into Mr. Shepherd's butt. Mr. Shepherd is our principal and he's always real grouchy. Sometimes he walks around the school at lunchtime to yell at kids for having fun, and, unfortunately for me, today was one of those days.

"*W*hoa there, young lady," Mr. Shepherd said. "You almost ran right over me!"

"Sorry," I said. "I didn't see you!"

"That's the trouble these days," Mr. Shepherd added. "You kids are too busy rushing from one place to the other. You need to learn to slow down and take your time!"

"Yes, Mr. Shepherd," I nodded. I wanted to tell him that

his big butt had just cost me my race with Katie, except I thought he might get mad and call my mom and dad, so I just kept quiet.

As I walked back to class, I could feel my face getting all hot and prickly again. Some of the older kids were still laughing at me, because I guess it kind of looked funny when I ran into Mr. Shepherd's butt. I think it was one of those times Mom says I'll look back at and laugh, except I don't think it'll ever be funny, because it was the day my life in the fifth grade was ruined!

lesson

8

*W*ith the weekend finally here, and only two days left until the track meet, I decided I had better come up with a plan on how I was going to beat Katie. I decided my only chance was to train as hard as I could and hope it would be enough to win Tuesday's race. Quietly, I snuck downstairs and grabbed one of Mom's old exercise books off the bookshelf in Dad's office. I didn't want Mom and Dad to know that I was training for the race. I had never trained before, and I was sure that if they saw me, they'd start asking me a bunch of questions like: Why are you training so hard? Are you trying to beat Katie? Did you apologize like we told you to? Do you think we were born yesterday? Parents are always asking questions they already know the answer to.

I went back to my room and began to flip through the pages of the book. Each page had a pencil drawing of a woman doing a different exercise. Above each picture were words like "bum crunch," "tummy tuck," "donkey kick," and "leg burn." It all sounded a little strange and a little painful to me, but I figured it would probably help me get in shape for the big race. For the next hour, I did leg squats, arm curls, and side twists.

When I was done, I made my way to the backyard. I peeked through the hole in the fence to make sure my next door neighbor's dog was outside. Violet was quietly sleeping on the Grimsons' back deck. Over the years, Chris and I had developed a way of testing how long it took us to do things. We calculated our speed by counting Violet's barks.

50 jumping jacks = 15 Violet barks

10 cartwheels = 12 Violet barks

7 somersaults = 9 Violet barks

I knew that it took me thirteen Violet barks to make it around the backyard five times. If I could do it under thirteen, then I'd be ready for the race. I got myself into my runner's stance and called for Violet. I could hear her dog tags clinking together as she came off the deck and ran toward the fence. As soon as she barked, I started to run. I counted her barks as I made my way around the backyard. One ... two ... three ... I was right on track. I kept counting as I ran: four ... five ... six ... seven. I was nearly finished my fourth lap: eleven ... twelve ... thirteen. Thirteen? I wasn't even finished my fourth lap and Violet was already at bark number thirteen? I ran faster: sixteen ... seventeen ... eighteen ... nineteen. Nineteen! I collapsed on the grass. No wonder I had lost to Katie. I couldn't even make it around the backyard in thirteen Violet barks.

Defeated and a little tired, I went back to my room. It was no use. It would take a miracle for me to win Tuesday's race. It was either that or a giant meteor hitting Wellington Elementary and canceling school that day. I figured there was a better chance of a miracle happening than a meteor, but I prayed for both anyway.

lesson

9

*W*hen Sunday finally rolled around, I had given up any hope of a miracle or a meteor happening. I did my best to keep busy and not think about Tuesday. I helped Mom do the laundry and Dad wash the car. I even helped Chris weed the garden. Yet, no matter how hard I tried, I couldn't stop thinking about the race or about Katie. The more I thought about it, the more I was sure Katie would be calling to apologize. After all, the fight had been mostly her fault. Only, guess what ... she didn't call. All Sunday, the phone rang exactly twelve times and none of the calls was from Katie.

Call #1   Grandma Mary called to see if Dad could come over to unplug her kitchen sink.

Call #2   Grandma Mary called again to see if Dad could pick up some butter, skim milk, and eggs on his way to unplug the drain.

Call #3   Some girl named Lucy called for my disgusting brother. She was probably calling to find out how he got to be soooo ugly.

Call #4   My mom's best friend Linda called. She invited us over to her house for dinner, but Mom said we couldn't make it, because Dad was at Grandma's and would be there a long time. I'm kinda glad she said no, because Linda has a really weird son named Teddy. He's six years old and likes to pick his nose and eat it. It's very disgusting.

Call #5   That girl Lucy called for Chris again. I listened in on the call for a few minutes, but hung up when I heard her tell him he was so cute. Gross me out! She must be blind or something!

Call #6   Dad called to ask Mom to look up the number for the plumber who unplugged the toilet after I flushed the orange down it.

Call #7   Wrong number. It was an old lady trying to order Chinese food.

Call #8   Auntie Marlene called to talk to Mom. Mom says
           Auntie Marlene needs to find a hobby, because
           she spends too much time dressing up her two
           miniature poodles, Gilbert and Sullivan, like
           characters from famous movies. She likes to take
           pictures of them and send them to all her relatives.
           We have a whole photo album full of these
           pictures. My favorite is a picture of Gilbert and
           Sullivan dressed like the Tin Man and Scarecrow
           from *The Wizard of Oz*.

Call #9   Macy Daniels called to see if I had finished my
           math homework. I told her I had, but since Katie
           usually helped me with it and since we were no
           longer friends, I had to get my dad to help me, and
           he always gets the answers wrong.

Call #10   That dumb girl Lucy called again! She must really
           have rocks in her head or something, because she's
           been calling Chris *all* weekend long. I told Mom
           that Chris was talking to a girl, and she told me to
           mind my own business.

Call #11   Grandma Mary called to talk to Dad, but he and Mom were out at the grocery store, so I ended up talking to her for an entire hour! We talked about her hearing aid, the price of lettuce, and the clump of hair the plumber found in her drain.

Call #12   Auntie Marlene called again. She wanted to remind Mom to check her e-mail because she sent some new pictures of Gilbert and Sullivan. This time she dressed them up like Jack and Rose from *Titanic*. Mom sighed when she saw the pictures and said that Auntie Marlene is NUTS!

What a rotten weekend! It's all Katie's fault!

lesson

10

*E*ven though I didn't want to admit it, it was true ... Katie was faster than me! She had beaten me during gym practice and she had even beaten me the next day at lunch. Though I probably *could* have beaten her, if Mr. Shepherd's butt hadn't got in the way. The whole thing was making me feel terribly sick. So sick that I didn't even feel like eating dinner. Instead, I went straight to my room and crawled into my bed. Mom came in to see if I was feeling okay. I told her that I was nervous about the race on Tuesday. She told me that I would do just fine and that she and Dad would be proud of me no matter what. Mom is always telling me dumb stuff like that. I bet if I told her the whole world was going to explode, she'd still say, "That's okay, P.J., things will be better tomorrow!"

Mom had only been gone a few minutes when Dad came into my room.

"Your mom tells me you're nervous about the race on Tuesday," he said. "Do you want to talk about it?"

"Not really!" I said, pulling my blankets up over my head.

"You know, it's normal to be a little nervous. Everyone feels like that from time to time."

Why does my dad always ask me questions like, "Do you want to talk?" or "Do you think I'm made of money?" or "Do I look like I was born yesterday?" and then when I answer him, he ignores me, kind of like I never said anything at all. It's weird.

"You're not still upset about Katie, are you?"

I didn't answer him, because I thought it was better to be silent than to lie.

"You apologized on Friday like we told you to … right?"

Without even looking, I could tell he was mad.

"P.J.!" he shouted.

I looked out from beneath my blankets long enough to shake my head.

"Why didn't you say you were sorry?" he asked.

"I was going to, but then Katie turned the whole class against me!"

"No one cares whether you win the race or not!" Dad said in his most serious voice. "I don't know why you won't believe me. Your mother and I have both told you that. We would be proud of you whether you won a ribbon or not."

He got up from my bed and patted me on the lump he thought was my head.

"I know you'll do the right thing tomorrow," he said.

I lay under my covers for a few seconds, just to make sure he was actually gone before I sat up. Alone in my room, I realized Dad was right! It didn't matter if I won the race, as long as I tried my best. And besides, I really missed Katie.

I was feeling really good about everything and was just about to go to sleep, when someone knocked on my door. I knew it had to be my brother Chris, because Mom and Dad never knock. I closed my eyes and pretended like I was sleeping, so he'd go away. I figured he just wanted to come in and tease me for being such a big baby. When I didn't answer him, he opened my door and walked over to my bed. I sat up real fast, just in case he was going to do something like draw a mustache on my face, or stick my hand in warm water so I'd pee the bed.

"I knew you were faking!" he said.

"I was not!" I shouted.

"Whatever you say," he laughed. "I guess you don't want my help with that problem you've been having at school."

He turned around and started to walk out of my bedroom.

"What kind of help?" I asked. I still planned on apologizing, but decided I didn't want to be rude, so I'd listen to what he had to say.

"I know how you can win the race on Tuesday!"

"Dad says it's not important whether I win or not. He said it's just about doing the best I can do." I said.

"Yeah, I figured he'd tell you something like that," Chris said, nodding his head. "Parents are pretty weird when it comes to this kinda thing. They're not the ones who have to go to school every day and have the kids call them 'Slow Poke Parker.' But if you want to do what Dad says, that's okay with me."

I thought about it for a second and then said, "No, I'd like to hear your idea."

Chris looked back at the door to make sure Mom and Dad weren't there, then sat down on my bed. He got this serious look on his face and leaned in real close.

"Now, if I tell you how to win, you have to promise not to tell another living soul, not even Mom or Dad!" he whispered.

"Why not?" I whispered back.

"Because it's a major secret that only the best athletes in the world know about!" he answered. "Have you ever heard of Babe Ruth or Mickey Mantle?"

I shook my head.

"Those guys were two of the greatest baseball players that ever lived!" he said. "They knew about this top-secret thing and used it all the time!"

"What is it?" I shouted, because I was super excited.

"Quiet, you idiot!" Chris snapped. "If Mom and Dad come in, then I can't help you!"

"Sorry," I whispered.

"It's a special drink that gives your muscles a turbo boost.

You have to take it one day before the race, so your muscles have time to energize," he explained.

"Does it work?" I asked.

"At the start of baseball season last year, I was in a horrible slump," he said. "I couldn't hit a thing! I took one drink of this and ended up hitting four home runs during the next game. I finished the season with the most RBI'S and was given the MVP trophy at our final game!"

"Does it taste gross?" I hoped he would say it tasted like a strawberry milkshake, because I love strawberry milkshakes.

"Yeah, it's pretty gross, but if you plug your nose you can't taste it," he said.

I sat quietly and thought about it for a moment. It all sounded good, except for the gross-tasting part, but then I decided it couldn't be any worse than some of Mom's cooking.

"How do I know you're not trying to play a trick on me or something?" I asked him. "What if it makes me sick or gets me in trouble or makes me look stupid. Like the time you told me to tell my teacher that thunder comes from two clouds bumping into each other."

"Because you're my little sister, dimwit!" he said. "I'm also the person who taught you how to ride your bike and tie your shoes. Besides, if you lose the race on Tuesday, everyone will know I'm related to a loser!"

It wasn't a nice answer, but it sounded like Chris, so I figured he must have been telling the truth.

"Okay, I'll try it!" I said.

He reached into his pocket and pulled out a crumpled-up piece of paper. He placed it in my hand and then leaned forward to give me one last piece of advice.

"After Mom and Dad go to bed, sneak downstairs and make the drink. You should drink it right away, too, because the quicker you take it, the more time it has to work."

He got up from my bed and left the room. I held the paper in my hands for a bit, then carefully opened it and began to read it out loud.

Christopher Parker's Top Secret Recipe for Athletes Only!!!

½ cup of orange juice

1 tsp of lemon juice

1 tbsp of soy sauce

4 tbsp of mayonnaise

1 tsp of vinegar

2 drops of ketchup

4 drops of mustard

½ cup of pickle juice

2 tsp of horseradish

a pinch of salt and pepper

and a dash of cayenne pepper for color

Stir all the ingredients together with a spoon and drink immediately.

Later that night, once I was sure Mom and Dad were asleep, I snuck down to the kitchen. I mixed up the drink and looked at it in the glass. It looked like pink mud and smelled like smelly gym socks. I picked up the glass, plugged my nose, and drank the whole thing. It was lumpy and slimy and tasted horrible! I took a deep breath and then waited. I wondered if my muscles would feel different right away.

It didn't take long before I felt something, except it wasn't my muscles – it was my stomach! It felt like my stomach was doing somersaults. The whole room started to sway. I ran out of the kitchen and straight for the bathroom. I was sick, really, really sick.

lesson 11

I spent all of Monday in bed because whenever I got up, I threw up! Mom brought me "sick food" like soup and Jell-O, and she even let me drink ginger ale and eat ice cream in bed. I told Mom and Dad about Chris's secret recipe and he got in major trouble! Dad made him come in and say he was sorry, and he cried when he did! I think he felt really bad because I could have died and everything! Dad asked me if I had finally learned my lesson, and I told him that I had. I said that I would never believe a single thing Chris ever told me again! Dad said that wasn't the lesson I was supposed to learn. He explained the lesson to me for about an hour and said that if I didn't apologize to Katie, I was grounded! I promised.

lesson

12

*H*aving almost died made me realize how much I missed Katie, not to mention Dad said I'd be grounded if I didn't. So I apologized first thing Tuesday morning. Katie was really good about the whole thing.

"It's okay, P.J.," she said. "I knew you'd apologize eventually."

"So, are we still best friends?" I asked.

"Of course," she smiled. "But can you promise me something?"

"Sure," I answered. "What?"

"If I win the race today, can you promise not to get mad?" Katie asked.

"I promise I won't get mad," I said. "I've moved on from running anyway. I'm totally into jumping rope now! Did you know I can jump 163 times without even stopping? I think that may be a new record."

"That's great, P.J.," Katie said.

We were just about to enter our classroom, when Katie stopped suddenly.

"Want to know a secret?" she asked.

"Sure," I said.

"Well, I sort of had this idea that you and I could both win the race this afternoon. Do you want to know how?"

I felt kind of nervous because my stupid brother had that same exact look on his face when he told me his idea.

"If I have to drink something gross, then I don't want to do it," I said.

"No, it's nothing like that!" she laughed. "I was thinking that if we ran together and crossed the finish line at the same time, then we would both get a first-place ribbon. That way, we'd both win!"

I could tell she was really proud of her idea, because she started twisting her hair on her finger. She always does that when she gets an answer right in class.

"You'd do that for me?" I asked.

"Sure!" she said. "That's what best friends are for!"

I was so excited I could hardly wait until the race. Katie and I couldn't stop laughing all morning because we had a secret no one else knew about. We stopped laughing after Ms. Watkins gave us her "I've had enough" look. My mom has that same look when I ask too many questions.

During lunch, we practiced crossing the finish line at the same time. It was pretty hard because sometimes I felt like running ahead and beating Katie, even though we had decided we wouldn't do that! After lunch, we got changed into our gym clothes and headed out to the field. There were kids everywhere! I even saw my dumb brother doing the long jump. He fell in the dirt face first and everyone laughed at him. It was great!

"Okay, girls," Ms. Watkins shouted. "I need all the girls to line up behind the white line. When I blow my whistle, you can start the race. The first girl to cross the finish line, where the orange flag is, wins!"

My heart started beating really hard. Katie grabbed my hand and squeezed it. All the girls lined up on the white line. There were only seven of us, because Macy Daniels was home sick.

"On your mark!" Ms. Watkins yelled. "Get set ... go!"

I don't even remember hearing Ms. Watkins blow her whistle. I started running as fast as I could. Katie was right beside me. I turned and smiled at her and she smiled back. For the entire race we ran side by side. Then, as we got near the finish line, something really weird happened. It was like my body was taken over by some strange force or something, because just as we were about to cross the finish line together, I got the sudden urge to run ahead and finish first. And unfortunately, that's kind of what I did!

After the race, Ms. Watkins came over to where I was standing. She was holding a small white envelope in her hands.

"Great job, P.J.!" she cheered. "That sure was a close race between you and Katie."

I looked around to see where Katie was, but couldn't find her anywhere. Ms. Watkins reached inside the envelope and pulled out three shiny ribbons. She handed me the blue ribbon and then gave Elizabeth Williamson the gold third-place ribbon.

"Where's Katie?" Ms. Watkins asked. "I have her second-place ribbon. Has anyone seen her?"

"I think I saw her run up to the school," Claire Kippen shouted. "Maybe she had to use the bathroom."

"Thanks, Claire," Ms. Watkins smiled. "I'll just give this to her when we get back to class." She took the ribbon and put it back in the envelope. "I'd like everyone to move on to their next event."

As I walked across the field toward the long jump, I started to get that yucky ache in my stomach again. I held the ribbon tightly in my hand. I didn't want to pin it to my shirt because I knew I didn't win the race fair and square. I wanted to run after Katie and tell her I was sorry, but I was afraid she wouldn't speak to me. I took the ribbon and stuffed it into my pocket. Being first suddenly didn't feel so good.

lesson

13

*W*hen the track meet was over, we all went back to class. When I walked into the classroom, everyone was laughing. At first I didn't know what they were laughing about, until I looked up and saw it. There, on the chalkboard, was a picture of me with the words *P.J. Parker is a big fat cheater!* written across it. I knew Katie drew the picture, because she had white chalk dust all over her red T-shirt.

I walked up to the chalkboard and erased the picture before Ms. Watkins came in. When I sat back down at my desk, I turned around to look at Katie. I wanted to say I was sorry, but she wouldn't even look at me. I got up from my desk and walked over to her.

"Katie," I said. "I know you probably never want to talk

to me again, but I'm really, really sorry."

"You're right," Katie shouted. "I don't ever want to speak to you again! You're nothing but a big fat cheater!"

"I really didn't plan on winning," I explained. "It sort of just happened. It was like I was possessed or something."

"I thought you were my friend," Katie said. "I guess the only person *you* care about is yourself!"

Just then, Ms. Watkins entered the classroom. I had no choice but to go back to my desk.

"I'd just like to congratulate all of you for participating today at the track meet," she said. "Each of you displayed great sportsmanship and I was very proud of all of you. Great job!"

I felt like crawling under my desk. I pulled the ribbon from my pocket and looked at it. It wasn't beautiful anymore! It was ugly and awful. I had ruined everything. Katie didn't want to be my friend anymore, and all because of this stupid ribbon. Dad was right; I knew exactly what I had to do.

"Oh, I almost forgot!" Ms. Watkins said. "You didn't get your second-place ribbon, Katie. It's here in this envelope."

As Ms. Watkins handed Katie her red ribbon, I stood up and cleared my throat.

"Could I say something?" I asked. "It'll only take a second."

Ms. Watkins looked confused, but nodded her head anyway.

"I don't deserve my ribbon," I announced. The whole class looked stunned. "Katie and I were supposed to win the race together, but I acted like a big jerk and beat her."

I bit the inside of my cheek really hard so I wouldn't cry.

"I want to give my ribbon to Katie because she's the real winner," I continued. "And I also want to tell her that I'm really sorry for being such a terrible friend."

I walked over to Katie and put the ribbon on her desk. Then I went back to my desk and sat down. No one said anything for a really long time. Then Ms. Watkins said something.

"Sometimes people forget what's important," she said. "We tend to get focused on things that seem important at the time, but really aren't. And sometimes we get so focused on those unimportant things that we end up hurting people we care about. I think P.J. learned a very valuable lesson today.

Isn't that right, P.J.?"

I nodded my head.

"Now, can everyone please take out their math books and work on pages twenty-five to twenty-six until the bell rings."

lesson

(14)

*T*he bell seemed to take forever to ring. I couldn't get any of my math work done because all I kept thinking about was Katie. When the bell finally rang, I jumped out of my seat and ran straight to my locker. I didn't want to talk to anyone. I grabbed my jacket super fast and ran out the front door. I felt so horrible and embarrassed.

I wouldn't blame Katie if she never talked to me again, I thought to myself. Who would want to have a friend like me?

Just then I heard Katie's voice.

"Wait up, P.J.!" she yelled. "Wait for me!"

I looked behind me and saw Katie running as fast as she could. Her jacket was hanging from one arm and she was holding her backpack in her hands.

"I want to talk to you," she said.

I knew exactly what she was going to say. She was going tell me that I was a rotten friend and that she never wanted to speak to me again. I figured she might also tell me that she wanted her purple sweater back, because I borrowed it last winter. She'd also probably tell me that she wanted back all the stickers and friendship pins she had ever given me. Then I'd have to tell her that I lost her purple sweater, traded her stickers for gum, and used her friendship pins to fix a hole in my ripped slipper. There was no way this was going turn out well.

"I don't really want to talk," I said.

"Well, *I* do!" Katie said. "You know, you really hurt my feelings today, P.J."

"I know," I said.

"And I probably shouldn't even forgive you," she admitted. "But it took a lot of courage to stand up in class and say what you did in front of everybody!"

"I just wanted you to know how sorry I am," I said.

"I do know and I forgive you … for the second time," she laughed.

"So, does this mean we can be friends?" I asked.

"Of course," she smiled. "As long as you promise never to race me again."

"I promise," I said.

We walked silently for a while, until Katie suddenly stopped.

"Guess what?" she said.

"What?" I asked.

"I heard from Belinda Jones that Gary Fisher has a big crush on you!" she said.

"YUCK!" I shouted. "THAT'S SO GROSS!"

"Want to come to my house so you can hear what she told me?" Katie asked.

"Did your Mom do any baking?" I said.

"I think she made a chocolate cake today. We can have some when we get there," Katie smiled.

"Sounds great!" I shouted. "I'll race you."

interview
with
carolyn mctighe

Clearly you've observed the way pre-teen girls interact as you wrote this book. To what extent is the story a result of your observation of girls you know now, and to what extent is it based on memories of your own childhood?

Having a pre-teen daughter and seeing the sorts of things she and her little friends get into has certainly helped me with the development of the characters in this book. The story itself though, is actually from my own childhood. When I was in the third grade this very thing happened to me, and sadly I must admit I behaved much like P.J. The only difference between the two stories is that I didn't listen to my older brother's bad advice. The memories I have of grade school are not only some of my fondest memories, but are also some of my most vivid. I visited those memories quite often while writing this book.

The making of lists is a feature of this story. Why did you choose to use this device?

When I was a little girl I had a best friend named, Tricia. Tricia and I used to write notes to each other all the time. In fact, we did it so often that we ended up getting in trouble quite a bit from our teacher, Ms. Watkins. We wrote about everything on those lists and those lists contained information that, at the time, was very important to both Tricia and I.

Using lists throughout the book gave me the chance to reveal parts of the girls' personalities that couldn't be learned from just reading the story—private thoughts shared between two good friends. In learning these intimate details about P.J. and Katie, readers are better able to understand why each girl behaves the way she does. Plus, it's just a lot of fun to read!

Friendship is an important theme in your book. So how is it that best friends can fall out over what seems to be a minor misunderstanding?

Friendships are very complex relationships. When you think about children, it's easy to see how little misunderstandings can get blown out of proportion and result in the breakdown of a seemingly close friendship. When I was a little girl I can remember one of my closest friends getting mad at me, because I wouldn't share my chocolate chip cookies with her at lunch. We eventually resolved things, but at the time we were both very angry with one another. I can remember thinking that I didn't want to be friends with her anymore. When you're small your emotions are so close to the surface that they tend to get bruised very easily, which is exactly what happens to P.J. and Katie. From an adult perspective the girls are behaving childishly, but from their point of view this hiccup in their friendship is not only serious but completely justified.

In the end P.J. and Katie patch things up in their friendship. Do you think this kind of happy ending is within reach of girls who have these kinds of misunderstandings—or is it just your wish that they could do it?

Having been a young girl once, I know that girls are more than capable of patching up rifts and mending wounds that may be caused in friendships. The truth is, I honestly think that children are much better at forgiving and forgetting than adults are. I have seen my fair share of little girls, including my own daughter, get into big fights with their best friends, only to forget about it the next day. I've often thought that grown-ups could learn a thing or two from the relationships children have with their friends.

How do you go about choosing the stories you are going to write?

When it comes to picking stories that I want to write, I first have to feel that the story is worth telling. If I like the story and I like the characters in it, then I will invest the time in developing it further. There have been times though, where I've come up with a story idea and no matter how hard I try, I just can't make it work. Either the flow of the story isn't smooth, or the characters just don't come together like I want them to. When that happens, I put the story away in a desk drawer and revisit it a few months later to see if I can maybe salvage something from it. As for the stories themselves, I usually get my ideas from reading newspapers or watching movies. I also love to listen to stories that friends and family tell. You would be amazed at how many little gems you can find when you just open your ears and listen.

Carolyn McTighe is a freelance writer who has written for CBC Radio, the *Los Angeles Times, Toronto Sun, Ottawa Sun, 24 Hours Vancouver* and *ELLE Canada*. She is also author of *The Sakura Tree*. Carolyn lives in Alberta with her husband and four children.